Lisa Rita is a woman of great faith and believes that you can follow your dreams through the faith of God. She loves writing and hopes to produce a memoir one day in order to help those who have gone through rough times. Lisa also loves dancing, playing the drums and martial arts. She would love children to experience joy through her books and enjoy reading them. She is hoping to publish her books in order to benefit others and hopes they will enjoy them too. This is her aim. She believes everybody is given a gift from God to use and present it to the world. Nobody should ever give up; follow your heart and you'll make it happen. Lisa wants to ensure everybody that they can make it by the grace of God.

DANCING DOLPHINS

LISA RITA

Austin Macauley Publishers™

LONDON ● CAMBRIDGE ● NEW YORK ● SHARJAH

A CIP catalogue record for this title is available from the British Library.

ISBN 9781528996747 (Paperback)
ISBN 9781528996754 (ePub e-book)

www.austinmacauley.com

First Published (2021)
Austin Macauley Publishers Ltd
25 Canada Square
Canary Wharf
London
E14 5LQ

Dedicated to my wonderful children, Isaac and Julia, and the rest of my beautiful family. God bless!

I'd like to thank my daughter, Julia, for the idea of a dolphin getting caught in a net; this is where I got the idea from.

"Let's go fishing, Mum," Flipper said eagerly.

"Yes, good idea," Flipper's mum, Phillipa, replied, "We need to get a good feed before our dance concert later on."

The pair of dolphins were to perform a dance concert together to celebrate Donald Dolphin being rescued, after he had beached himself recently.

Donald beached himself after his partner, Donna dolphin, had died. He was very sad.

But luckily, he was spotted by a pair of beachgoers and was pushed back out to sea.

His friends, Flipper and Phillipa, were trying to cheer Donald up and welcome him back to the sea world. But they needed to catch some fish before their big performance.

So, they swam off together searching for a feed.

Flipper was so excited he started practising his dance flips on the way.
"Look how high I can flip, Mum!" Flipper boasted.
"That's why I named you Flipper!" His mum smiled.
"Watch me twirl," Flipper said as he began twirling around and around.
"Watch out, Flipper!" his mum warned.
But Flipper did not notice the shark nets ahead of him, and continued twirling right into them.
"Oh no," Phillipa said, "You're entangled in the nets."
"Help, Mum! They're wrapped all around me."
His mum desperately tried to untangle the nets with her nose. But Flipper had managed to wrap the nets around himself so tightly, it was impossible for her to untangle them herself.

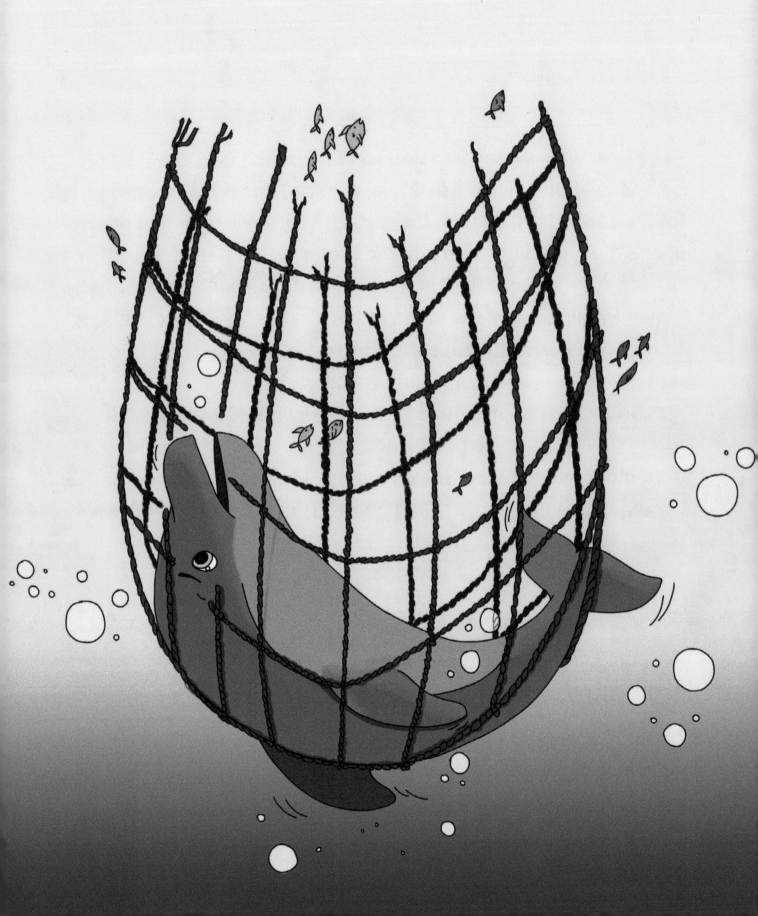

"The only way we can free you from these nets is to cut them off."
"Go and get Sally Swordfish, Mum, she'll cut me out. We can't be late for the concert. I'll float on the surface to breathe until you return."
Flipper's mum quickly swam into the ocean to find Sally Swordfish. But she wasn't in her usual fishing spot.
Then Phillipa heard the violin playing, "Yes, of course, Sally is practising her violin nose with the rest of the sea creatures for the concert later."
She followed the sound of the music and found them all practising together.
"Very nice melody fellow sea creatures," Phillipa complimented. "But could you kindly excuse Sally Swordfish for a moment, please? It's an emergency."
"What's wrong?" Sally asked.
"It's Flipper, he's stuck in the local shark nets. I need your sharp sword nose to cut him out please."

"Okay, Okay, I 'll follow you," Sally Swordfish said soaring through the ocean behind Phillipa.
They heard Flipper squealing in distress in the distance.
"Something 's wrong, let 's go quickly," Phillipa asserted.

In the meantime, Shawn the Shark had sensed Flipper in distress and followed his distress signals.

"What a tasty little treat," he muttered to himself, "All wrapped up like a present just for me. They don't call these shark nets for no reason."

"Hey little fellow, I'll set you free." Shawn the Shark smiled with his sharp pointy teeth.

"Go away," Flipper squealed.

Shawn the Shark opened his mouth widely.

"Over there!" Phillipa instructed and Sally Swordfish charged into Shawn the Shark with her pointy nose.
"Ouch." Shawn yelped. He didn't know what had hit him.

He swam around and saw Sally Swordfish glaring at him.
"Stop poking your nose into other fish's business," Shawn said as he
swam off.

Flipper was crying, "Mum, he was trying to eat me!"
"It's okay now, we are here to free you," Phillipa calmed him down.
"At least my long sharp nose is good for something," Sally Swordfish
said as she carefully cut Flipper free.
Flipper was freed and had finally settled down. His mum reassured him,
"If we leave now, we can still make it back in time for
Donald's concert."
"Yippee!" Flipper cheered. They all swam back to join the other
sea creatures.

As they were approaching the orchestra of sea creatures, they heard, "Get into position! Donald's coming."

Olly the Octopus was ready with all her eight tentacles on the piano keys. The sea horses were playing the trumpets with their noses. Sally got her violin nose ready and crab had his nippers on his guitar strings. Flipper and Phillipa swam in the middle of the instruments and took their dance positions.

Donald arrived and they all started performing.

Sally commenced playing her nose with the violin gently. Then Olly joined in with an amazing performance with all her arms playing on the piano. Then the seahorses began tooting their trumpet noses and Crab played an electrifying performance on his guitar.

Flipper and his mum danced in the middle of the orchestra, flipping and twirling around like ballerinas. Finally, they ended the show with a somersault. All the clams clapped, as did Donald, clapping with his flippers.
Donald wanted to join in. He wanted to dance too. So, he joined the circle and the dolphins continued flipping around like crazy!

Even Shawn the Shark wanted to know what all the noise was about. He observed from a distance, "Flippin' mad," he commented, and he shook his tail and swam off.

Then Flipper and Phillipa invited Donald for a surf in the waves.
They all jumped and rode through the waves joyfully.
"You certainly know how to cheer up an old dolphin!" Donald smiled.

After all the dancing and surfing Donald was tired and headed
for their seabeds.
As Flipper, his mum and Donald drifted off, Flipper reassured Donald,
"Remember you 'll always have us."
"Thank you kindly," Donald responded, "Sea you in the morning."
He blinked.
And they all drifted off to sea—leep.

The End...

Printed in Australia
Ingram Content Group Australia Pty Ltd
AUHW012358060923
383323AU00027B/157